To my daughter Colleen, who helped me imagine this story
—J.G.

To all the hardworking, patient, inspiring,
and dedicated teachers
—R.C.

Marley Goes to School
Text and art copyright © 2009 by John Grogan

Printed in the U.S.A.

Library of Congress Cataloging-in-Publication Data is available.
ISBN 978-0-06-156151-1 (trade bdg.) — ISBN 978-0-06-156152-8 (lib. bdg.)

Typography by Jeanne L. Hogle
09 10 11 12 13 LP/LPR 10 9 8 7 6 5 4 3 2 1
❖
First Edition

John Grogan

Marley Goes to School

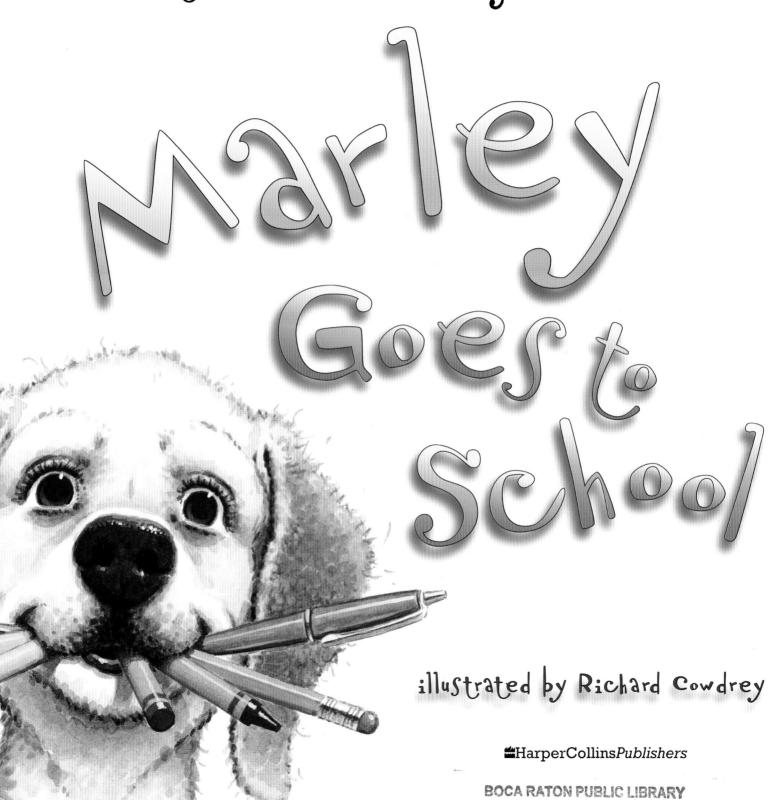

illustrated by Richard Cowdrey

HarperCollinsPublishers

It was the first day of school, and Cassie laid out her back-to-school supplies.

Pencils. Check.

Crayons. Check.

Ruler. Check.

Paper. Check.

Marley was all set for the big day too.

By the front door, he laid out his supplies.

Chew bone. Arf!

Squeaky toy. Woof!

Liver treats. Ruff!

Favorite blanket. Awooo!

Baby Louie crawled around the corner. "Waddy go school too!" he exclaimed.

Mommy looked at Marley thumping his tail by the front door. "I don't think so, Big Guy," she said.

"I definitely don't think so," added Daddy.

"You silly dog," Cassie said, patting Marley on his big blocky head. "School's for kids, not dogs."

Marley cocked his head and let out a low whine.
Cassie was his best friend, and he was used to
going everywhere she went. To the park.
To the playground. To Grandma's house.

Even to bed!

"Grab your backpack," Mommy called out. "We don't want to be late."

"Arf! Arf!" Marley said, grabbing his leash in his teeth and hopping up on his hind legs and dancing by the door.

"Arf! Arf! yourself," Mommy said. "You're going in the backyard where you can't get into trouble."

"Good idea," said Daddy, and the whole family set off to walk Cassie to school.

Marley did not stay in the backyard for long. He started to dig. And he dug and dug and dug. And the dirt flew up behind him until it formed a giant pile, a regular Mount McMarley. Up flew Mommy's marigolds. Out flopped Daddy's daffodils. Away went Cassie's carrot patch. Soon he had cleared a nice, cozy tunnel under the backyard fence. With a wiggle and a waggle and a whip-whop of his tail, he belly-crawled to freedom.

Marley sniffed his way to the sidewalk, looked both ways—*All clear!*—and followed Cassie's scent straight to the front door of the school.

The front door was propped open. *They're expecting me!* Marley thought, and he walked right in.

Down the hallway he trotted, stopping in each room in search of his beloved Cassie.

Marley tried the copy center. *Hmmm, not in here*, he thought, and then he took a moment to leave a calling card.

He tried the cafeteria, where the cooks were busy making lunch. He did not find Cassie, but Marley found the next best thing: a heaping pile of juicy hot dogs. *Well, I don't mind if I do!*

"Hey! You're not supposed to be in here!" one of the lunch ladies yelled. "Shoo! Go home!"

"Burrrrp!" answered Marley . . .

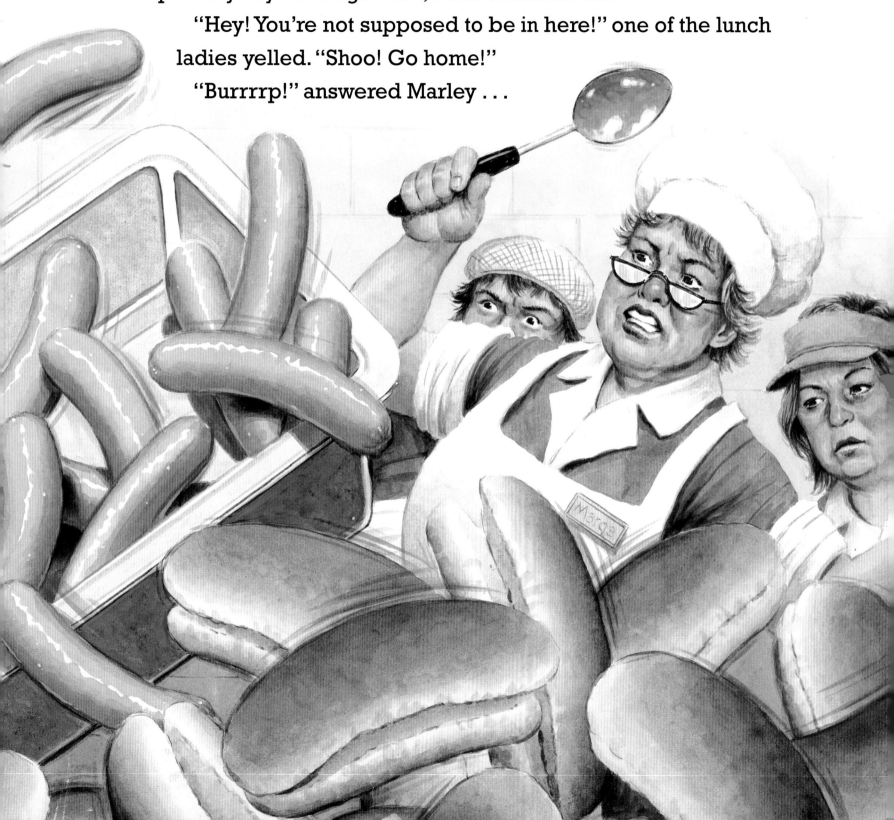

. . . and he trotted over to music class, where the orchestra was warming up. *Hmmm, she's not here either*, thought Marley, and then he joined the band for a song.

In science class, Marley did not find Cassie, but he did find a cage with ten white mice inside. *What are you doing in there?* With a scratch of his paw and a flip of his nose, Marley busted open the cage door and the mice scampered to freedom. He barked excitedly as if to ask, "Who wants to help me find Cassie?"

Marley followed the mice to the library, where the quiet didn't last long.

"Mice!" screamed a little girl.

"Big fat ones!" shouted a little boy.

Marley raced to the gymnasium, where he suddenly forgot all about Cassie. When that dog saw a ball, he could think only one thing: *Catch me if you can!*

"Hey!" yelled the teacher.

"Hey!" yelled the kids.

"Come back with our ball!"

But Marley did not come back. He streaked down the hall, skidded around the corner, did a somersault, and slid right into Mrs. Weatherbee's math class. Mrs. Weatherbee peered through her thick glasses as she wrote on the chalkboard.

Oh my," she announced. "We've just received a report of a wild animal on the loose in our school. If you come across this animal, stay back. He may be dangerous."

"Yes, Mrs. Weatherbee," the students said.

"Has anyone seen him?"

"No, Mrs. Weatherbee," the students said.

But they had seen him . . .

. . . and helped make sure that Mrs. Weatherbee would not. When the bell rang, Marley's ears perked up. Outside, he heard the happy shrieks of children playing. There was no sound Marley loved more than the sound of children at play. He headed toward it.

"Not so fast, Buddy Boy." The voice came from behind him. Gulp! It was Principal Peabody. She seized Marley by the collar and read his tag. "Aha! Cassie's dog. I should have figured."

She tied Marley to the radiator with a rope. "Face the corner," she said. "I'm calling your parents."

But when Principal Peabody returned two minutes later, all she found was half a rope, wet with dog drool. "Drat!" she said.

"There he goes!" shouted Vice Principal Tanner. "He's heading to the playground!"

"I'll head him off," cried the gym teacher.

"I'm on his tail!" declared Mrs. Weatherbee, shaking her fists.

"Tackle him!" screamed the lunch ladies.

The grown-ups chased Marley across the playground. They chased him through the tunnel and over the tires and under the hoops. They chased him up the jungle gym and down the slide. They chased him past the swing set and around the teeter-totter.

They chased him right into Cassie's arms.

"Marley!" Cassie shrieked with delight. "You did come to school!"

"Is that your dog?" Vice Principal Tanner asked.

"Um," Cassie said. "He looks somewhat familiar."

"There you are!" Mommy and Daddy yelled.

"Bad dog, Marley!"

"Bah boo boo, Waddy!"

Baby Louie said.

"Now, now," said Principal Peabody, "all's well that ends well." And Marley was so happy he jumped in the air and gave the principal a big, fat, sloppy kiss right on the lips.